Daniel Silverhawk

T0132079

The Puppy in Disguise

Print information available on the last page

Rev. date: 02/19/2019

To order additional copies of this book, contact:
Xlibris
1-888-795-4274
www.Xlibris.com
Orders@Xlibris.com

The Puppy in Disguise

Daniel Silverhawk

Once upon a time there was a cute little pup
Who thought she was ugly so she liked to dress up

She just couldn't believe she looked as cute as she did
So she created some masks and behind them she hid
Whatever she saw that would reflect how she felt
She created a costume she could wear like a belt

Her costumes were simple though some were quite funny
Like one Easter Sunday she dressed up like a bunny

The folks that she met knew she was wearing a mask
But they didn't know why so they never did ask
But the puppy was cute so the people were kind
They would pat her little head then pay her no mind

One day she was disguised as a dangerous bear
Putting the town on alert and creating a scare
She just wanted to scare the other dogs around town
Which she did with the courage to refuse to back down

Her mom called her home to protect from harm
But the puppy's simple plan had worked like a charm
She planned it all out from pattern to suit
And she wore the bear costume with claws in the boot

The puppy decided to turn it into a game
To disguise her true feelings and mask her deep shame

She learned to communicate and trick those around
To get what she wanted became easily found

She could dress like a kitten to get some milk in a bowl
She would purr and meow and scratch on a pole

Or dress like a raccoon when she wanted burgers to eat
She wore a lone ranger mask and could stand on two feet

She would dress up as a skunk to keep others away
She couldn't wear the smell but the stripes made her day
She even dressed like a pig once or twice as she dared
Not to roll in the mud but to prove no one cared

Then she created a costume to express her true thoughts
She dressed up as a puppy full of ugly black spots
This would be her best costume when facing the worst
Of all the costumes she made she would choose this one first.

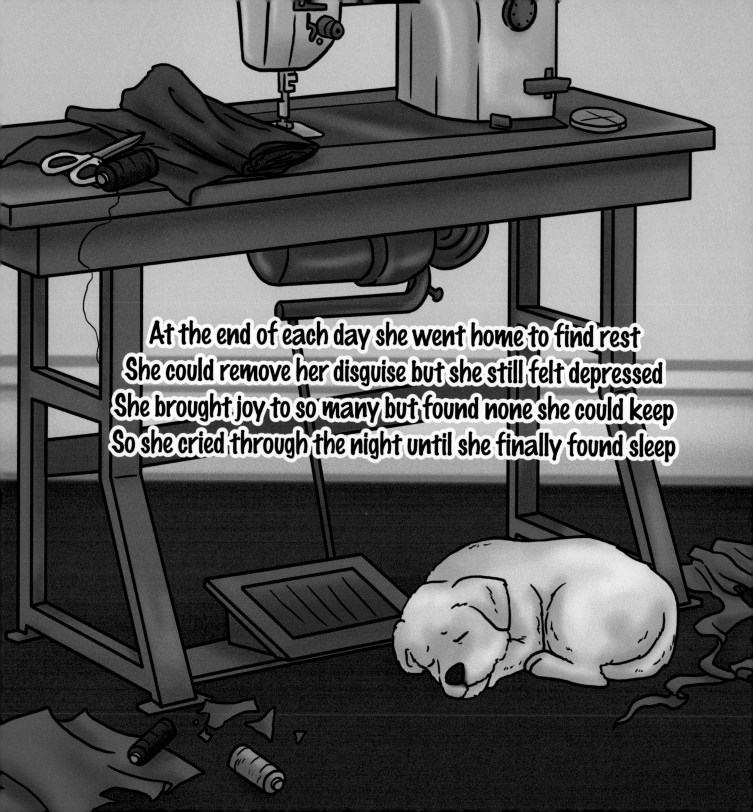

At the end of each day she went home to find rest
She could remove her disguise but she still felt depressed
She brought joy to so many but found none she could keep
So she cried through the night until she finally found sleep

She felt helpless and tired and desired a change
But that kind of disguise would certainly look strange
Whatever she tried only upset her far more
So she threw out all her costumes and lay flat on the floor

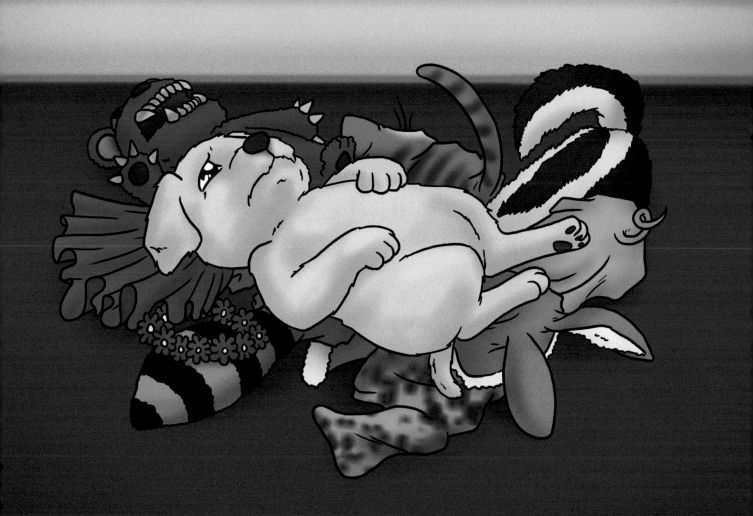

Then the pastor of the church was just passing by
When he saw the cute puppy he just wanted to cry

"What's the matter little puppy," the pastor did ask,
"You look so much cuter without any such mask"

The puppy felt the pastor
must not understand
As he offered a snack from
the palm of his hand
He encouraged the puppy to
take one little bite
But the puppy refused, it just
wouldn't feel right

So the pastor came closer to check for a cause
Of illness or injury or a thorn in her paws
When he looked in her eyes he noticed a tear
And the pain she was feeling was suddenly clear

Then the pastor did something the puppy didn't expect
He pulled a mirror from his pocket to let the puppy reflect
When she saw her reflection it opened her eyes
She saw a cute little puppy who was indeed very wise

Now the cute little puppy loves the life that she lives
She finds pleasure in helping and the hope that she gives
Creating nice outfits to show off her new views
The look of true beauty with a talent she can use

With no costumes, disguises or masks on the shelf
The cute puppy found happiness just being herself

So to all you cute puppies who just want to hide
The real beauty you show comes from the inside
Your appearance makes you beautiful, we all know that's true
But your actions make you beautiful inside your heart too

Now the costumes she makes let's everyone see
She is happy and joyful, exciting and free.

The beginning...

Printed in the United States
By Bookmasters